THE
TOURISTS

Hmmm!

Not bad but, Hmmm.

THE
TOURISTS

JULIANNE PACHICO

DAUNT BOOKS

First published in 2014 by
Daunt Books
83 Marylebone High Street
London W1U 4QW

1

ISBN 978 1 907970 67 2

Typeset by Antony Gray
Printed and bound by TJ International

www.dauntbooks.co.uk

To my parents

THE
TOURISTS

WHO'S COMING TO THE PARTY?
A lot of people, it's going to be a big
success: the Mendozas and the Vasquezes,
the Lorenzos and the Smiths. The maids
drag the white plastic chairs into the yard,
forming half-circles beneath the mango
tree and around the barbecue pit. The
gardeners carry out the big wooden table,
a security guard following closely behind
with a ruler to scrape off the white globs
of dried candlewax, accumulated in thick
layers from weeks of blackouts. The dogs
yip excitedly, nipping at people's ankles,
and behind the safety of their chickenwire
cage the rabbits look on, horrified. Inside
the kitchen, staring out the window, one
of the cooks says, 'We really need to lock
them up. Can you imagine Lola rolling

in her poo and then licking Mrs Montoya's hand?'

The caterers have arrived; they're getting set up. They're carrying big metal pans, steam rising beneath the lids, filled with white fish soaked in lemon juice, red peppers for the grill, raw bloody steaks and chicken breasts stabbed with fork marks. Nothing is extravagant, nothing is over the top, except for maybe the lobster claws on ice, the tins of caviar and the oysters that the cooks are busily prying open with their special metal knives. That's not his style.

Here he comes. Folding the cuff of his black shirt above his wrists so that a pale strip of unburnt skin shows, like a patch of exposed land on a jungle hillside. People rarely notice, but the three middle fingers of his right hand end abruptly in smooth pink stumps, neatly aligned with the humble pinkie. 'Looking good,' he says to the blinking white Christmas lights hanging from the branches of the grapefruit tree. 'Excellent,' he says while strolling past the arts and crafts supplies set out for the children by the pool: crayons and candles and paper plates. 'Go along now,' he says to one of the many cats, sitting on the drainpipe above the jacaranda bush, a distasteful expression behind its droopy whiskers. Who knows how many pets they have at this point? Just the other week he saw a turtle lumbering under the sofa in the living room, but when he got down on his knees to check there was nothing there, not even dust balls or coffee-flavored candy wrappers.

He wanders inside the house through

the swinging patio door, scratching the back of his neck. The maids have done a good job at making everything seem presentable. The bookshelves have been dusted, the broken electric piano cleared away (a lizard got electrocuted deep inside its mechanical guts years ago and ever since it's refused to make a sound, not even when the cats frantically chase each other across the black and white keys). Considering that they only come out to this country ranch every few months, for Easter or holiday weekends, the house still feels fairly lived in: the living room fresh-smelling with the sharp scent of white laundry powder, the lampshades shiny without a single dead moth smear, no cobwebs around the chandelier or shelves of VHS tapes.

'How's it going?' he says, knocking on

the door to his daughter's room at the same time that he pushes it open. The room is deserted – the only sign of her presence is a stack of CD cases spilled all over the bed, next to some shredded packets of plantain chips. It's hard to restrain himself, this rare opportunity to intrude in her bedroom – normally the door is firmly locked, American bands screaming their angst-filled rage from her stereo on the other side. So he now finds his eyes flickering greedily, taking in one new poster after another hanging on the walls. The one of a mournful-eyed American singer with shaggy blond hair holding an acoustic guitar, that's definitely new; Snoopy dancing with a balloon, that's been up since she was in kindergarten and received it as a present at one of the immense birthday parties she hosted here for all her classmates. The closet doors are half open; he can glimpse the shelves lined with stuffed animals that couldn't fit into the storage trunk in the hallway, Care Bears and shabby dogs and other beasts that were never loved enough to be guaranteed a spot at their main house in Cali. There are rows of plastic toys based on countless American cartoon shows, Transformers and ThunderCats and Ghostbusters, stiff plastic bodies randomly positioned in a messy parade, silently poised with their daggers and ray guns, ready to leap into battle with invisible enemies at a moment's notice. Everything slowly gathering dust.

From where he's standing he can clearly see that the empty packets of plantain chips have been licked clean, not a single crumb remaining. Shaking his head, he

14

picks them up between two fingers and drops them from the bed onto the floor where it'll be easier for a maid to sweep them up. That's when he sees it – the small ziplock baggie lying on a pillow, half-filled with bright red Jell-o powder – the kind of treat you can purchase from street children at traffic lights. He picks it up and shakes it up and down, the powder accumulating at the bottom, except for the wet clumps clinging near the baggie's thin lips. He can already picture the garish stains across her front teeth and mouth, the demon red of her tongue flashing at the guests as she utters a sullen *hello*, the sticky finger smears on her shirt, running up and down the fabric as though a tiny animal with miniature bloody paws had danced all over her body. *Ave Maria,* the maids will say when they see her, closing their eyes in supplication. *Mija, what were you thinking? What will your father say when you show up looking like that for his party?*

The automatic gate rumbles at the same time that he hears car wheels crunching on the gravel driveway. He puts the JELL-O baggie in his back pocket, jammed tightly behind his cellphone. After closing the door behind him, he pulls his right shirt-sleeve down as far as it'll go, almost completely covering the white scars snaking over the backs of his hands.

Here they come. Black and blue high heels clicking, jackets draped over arms, wispy strands of thinning hair combed neatly back. The chauffeurs park the mud-splattered jeeps with Bogotá license plates under the fig trees; the bodyguards climb out and immediately cross their arms, already hovering in the background. He

waits under the mango tree in the back-
yard. Smoke rises from the barbecue pit.
The chefs grimly rotate sausages slashed
with deep knife cuts over the fire, red
peppers and onions impaled and sweating
on wooden sticks.

'Hello, hello,' he says in greeting. Right
hand hidden behind his back in a clenched
fist, left hand extended and welcoming,
fingers spread wide.

Everyone arrives safely, happily. Nobody's
been chased by the crazed spider monkey,
the one the maids have nicknamed 'Baloo'
for the size of his black testicles, so im-
pressively heavy that the housecleaners
whisper amongst each other: *now that's a
real man, Linda, just what you need, some-
one to keep you satisfied,* before exploding
into giggles. At the last big party (two years
ago? Three? Was it celebrating the successful

17

Congress run, or hosting the visiting HSBC managers?), Baloo had run back and forth over the stone wall for hours, staring hungrily at the food, the tables, and the guests most of all (this was before the shards of glass were installed along the wall's perimeter, before Uribe's successful presidential campaign based on vows to 'restore national peace and security', before he'd started hearing the clicking sounds of recording instruments every time he lifted the phone). At one point, Baloo had jumped down and stuck his head up Mrs Montoya's skirt, and her banshee screams had caused the maids in the kitchen to raise their eyebrows at each other.

Thankfully there's been no sign of Baloo for months now – the fact that the security guard has been tossing his slimy orange and banana peels into the forest, well away from the main house, has possibly helped. As a result the party is going well, the conversation gliding along smoothly, effortlessly. No bottles of *aguardiente* or rum yet, it's still early, the sun casting hazy yellow light over the freshly mown grass, the mosquitoes blessedly absent. Instead it's green glass bottles of chilled beer for the gentlemen, tall slender glasses of champagne for the ladies. The hired waiting staff stalk silently back and forth across the patio, black and white uniforms still free from wine splatters and crumbs. Everything is under control; everything is fine.

He doesn't see us, but we're watching.

We've been doing so for a while now. We didn't get any greetings, no gentle air kiss near the cheek, no firm pumping handshake, but that's okay, we don't take it personally, we don't mind. Instead we take our time, take things slow: there's no reason to rush, no reason to make things happen before they need to. We walk in slow circles around the barbecue pit, smelling the charcoal fire and crackling chicken skin with deep inhalations. We put our hands tentatively in the glass bowls of peanuts; what a nice rattling sound they make when we stir our fingers. We take turns gently touching the beer bottles, admiring the streams of condensation running down the smooth glass bodies. No one makes eye contact; nobody invites us to sample a plate of sliced limes or a tray of roasted garlic. But we're not upset; we're not bothered. For now, we're happy, watching the hummingbirds dart nervously amongst the orange flowerpots. Everything has been so tasteful, nothing over the top – no helicopters landing in the football field, no spray-tanned models greased up and wrestling each other while the guests cheer and look on. No one's slinging their arms around each other, singing classic Mexican *corridos* at the top of their lungs; no one's pulled the gun from their holsters and started shooting wildly at the darkening sky. Nothing like that. The food is delicious, and everyone is having a wonderful time.

He loves it when parties are at this stage – the post-beginning and pre-middle, when no one has gotten too drunk or noticed who's been pointedly ignoring them. It means he can sneak away to the bathroom adjoining his private bedroom, lock himself inside for up to fifteen minutes at a time, sometimes twenty. He sits on the bowl, chin resting in hands, trousers sagging around his ankles. It's moments like these when it's impossible to ignore: how all over his body there are patches of skin now drooping where they used to be firm and taut. There are brown and purple spots all over his arms that definitely weren't there twenty years ago either, and red moles on his upper shoulders he keeps mistaking for insect bites. This year, too, he suddenly found himself mentally adding secret descriptions to his friends' names: prostate-cancer Andrés; emphysema-cough Pablo; beet-juice-diet Mauricio. More and more lately, it seems as though everyone he knows is talking to doctors instead of priests, men with stethoscopes around their necks instead of crucifixes. He can't pinpoint the exact moment when it changed, but there's a new fear now lurking beneath everyone's low-volume conversations. It's not just extradition to Miami prisons or undercover DEA agents or stash house security guards secretly wearing wires beneath their collared shirts. It's also cancer cell counts, will-drafting, uneasy conversations with mistresses, even more uneasy conversations with wives. He's started biting his nails again too – they haven't been this short since he was seventeen, doing deliveries in the hillside neighbourhoods for local bosses. His first job. He would sit in the front seat for hours, waiting for his partner's signal, and tear off every last possible shred of nail, until the cuticles were non-existent.

(His right fingers were long back then too, with deliciously bitable nails – the index finger was his favorite).

But now's not the time to dwell on it. Not tonight. He pulls his trousers up briskly and rebuckles his belt. As usual, he flushes but doesn't wash his hands. He wanders past the bookshelves, back out to the porch. Under the drainpipe Mauricio is telling a story about his recent senatorial trip to Uruguay, how uncomfortable it made him to see all the small children at his official reception, the way they honoured his presence by saluting and marching across the basketball court, military dictatorship style.

'At least, if nothing else, we've never had that issue here,' he says, beer bottle coming dangerously close to clinking against his coffee-stained teeth. 'Long live democracy.'

By the mango tree Ravassa's wife is already drunk; he can tell by how closely she leans towards Alonso as he speaks, summarising a TV series about medieval knights in Spain that he's just finished watching. Alonso is half-Mexican, which maybe explains why he uses so many hand gestures while talking: the way he darts forward, parries, blocks, defends, you'd swear you could see the sword glowing in his hand, a luminescent silver. Ravassa's wife keeps laughing and reaching out, trying to brush her maroon-coloured nails against his chest.

The Rossi brothers are sitting in the white plastic chairs by the barbecue pit, smoking red-boxed Marlboros. When they make eye contact with him they both raise their hands at the same time like choreographed puppets, crooking their fingers in a *come-here* gesture. He shakes his head; he's not in the mood to discuss business. Not at the party; not here.

He turns away and merges with the group of children, huddled by the swimming pool. It only takes a quick scan of the crowd to see that his daughter's not among them: no long black braid hanging down her back, no baggy blue T-shirt with holes in the collar from her anxious chewing. His fingers brush briefly against the slight bulge in his back pocket from the JELL-O baggie. The children are all busy, hunched with intense focus over the paper plates. They're dripping crayon wax in the centre of the plates, creating a base that will harden and keep their candles propped up. The plates are then cast away into the swimming pool, transformed into tiny fragile boats, the orange flames casting faint reflections in the dark water below.

'Oh!' he shouts when one candle topples over and extinguishes with a mournful hiss. Some of the kids jump, startled by his cry; most simply turn slowly and stare. He tries to smile, even though he knows this never looks comforting: the scar splits his upper lip so that his tooth pokes out, a pink hairless line arches over his left eyebrow.

'It's fine,' one of the older girls says to a little boy she's been helping, whose eyes are getting bigger and more watery-looking by the second. 'Just make another one. What colour crayon do you want?' She shoves some into his fist.

He turns away, shoes crunching on the gritty patio tiles. He does this all the time: he'll bang his knee against the dining room table, or drop a tangerine onto the floor immediately after peeling it, or accident-ally fumble a fork, and then let out an explosive bellow of *OH!* It makes the maids come running, the bodyguards look up sharply. *Everyone keeps thinking you're having a heart attack,* his daughter once

27

told him, *but then it turns out you just spilled some milk.*

By now he's wandered over to the mango tree, where Alonso is still breathlessly summarising his beloved TV series to a circle of people. Alonso has the unfortunate skin type that turns as pink as strawberry juice, no matter the humidity levels or how slow he's been drinking.

'So they bring in the red-beard guy, begging and screaming,' Alonso is saying. 'But when the blade comes down, he doesn't cry out for his mother or wife or daughters. Instead he starts sobbing for his country, his army. *I did you wrong, I did you wrong,* he's shouting, and the crowd starts cheering.'

'Like the Romans,' says Ravassa's wife, lightly touching a small mark by her lower lip that she hopes nobody else has noticed –

a pimple? A mole? 'The Christians and the lions.'

At the border of the group, Mrs Montoya has just finished her story about Baloo, how he chased her around the yard, tugging on her skirt and smacking his thick black lips. 'Thank God they got rid of him,' she says, gesturing towards her feet. 'There's no way I could run in these heels.' Tom Harris and Robert Smith nod in unison, even though they're in separate departments at the fruit company (agronomy and marketing respectively) and don't really know each other that well. They're both secretly glad that Mrs Montoya's incessant chatter is filling in the silence between them. When she finally heads back to the patio to refill her drink, Tom shyly asks Robert if he has a lighter. Smoking together, looking at the pool and the squat orange flowerpots, the Christmas lights dangling like fireflies stuck in the grapefruit tree, Robert will tell Tom that Amanda Quintero's husband has just joined a strange new American religion that doesn't allow you to cut your hair.

'What will he do once it's summer?' Tom asks, who's only been here for six months and still sleeps with the fan as close to his bed as possible, blasting air in his face, even when it rains.

'Be hot,' says Robert, taking another drag.

He blows the smoke right into our faces, but we don't blink, we don't move an inch. We've been listening carefully, behaving ourselves, lingering on the edges. Sometimes we lean in close, inhale the faint scents of cologne and perfume, study the sweat on men's upper lips, the base of women's collarbones. An enormous black cicada buzzes past and hits the drainpipe with a clatter.

We're still watching him, too – the way he's rocking back and forth on his heels, rubbing his shirtsleeves as though chilled. 'Excuse me,' he says abruptly to one of the passing servers, a young woman holding a bowl scraped clean of lavender-flavoured goat's cheese. She immediately freezes in her tracks. 'My daughter – have you seen her?' He pauses, trying to find the right words for a description – the tip of her black braid, permanently wet from her nervous sucking? The damp patches in her armpits, regardless of the temperature? The scowling, baby-fat cheeks, the sour curdling of her mouth when he hesitantly says something like *You know, you could invite somebody over to spend the weekend – a friend of yours, if you'd like.* The icy cold feeling oozing from her shoulder blades as she contemptuously retreats to her room?

But the young woman is nodding her head, backing away, holding the bowl close to her chest like a shield. Right before she turns around, she says in a fast voice, 'By the palm tree, sir – Ramón was bringing her shrimp.' And just like that she flees across the patio, almost bumping into a flowerpot. As she disappears through the swinging door, he thinks, *Ramón?*

He turns and starts walking into the depths of the garden. He swings his arms purposefully, wrinkles his forehead with the expression of a man on a mission, so that anyone contemplating stopping him with a *Why so nice to see you, it's been ages!* will think twice. He pauses by the palm tree, resting his hand on the scars hacked into the trunk. They're ancient relics from his daughter's kindergarten birthday parties, epic affairs in which the garden filled with screaming children, waving plastic ThunderCats swords, their lips stained with bright blue frosting, the swimming pool transformed into a froth from their kicking legs and cannonball dives. *How about that friend of yours,* he'd said. *You used to invite him over here all the time. I don't think I've seen him in years. You know, the blond one?*

Dad, she'd said. *Why don't you shut the fuck up?*

On the ground is a solitary flip-flop, the grey ghost of her foot imprinted on the thin rubber. Nearby is a wooden stick smeared black from the grill, gnawed with teeth marks from where she scraped off every last piece of shrimp possible. He looks around, but the only eyes he meets are those of the rabbits, their trembling noses pushed up against the chicken wire, expressions the same as the young waitress moments before.

He walks ahead, leaving the flip-flop behind. He moves past the papaya trees, which have been afflicted by a mysterious disease for weeks now, the fruit stinking of rotten fish and the trunks covered in oozing sores. He passes the compost heap, filled with dry branches slashed from trees by the gardeners' sharp machetes, and kitchen scraps that the maids routinely carry out in orange plastic buckets. He walks by the abandoned birdhouse, vines hanging down the rotting wood, the lion cage with its rusty bars and leaf-covered roof. César the lion has been gone for half a decade, the peacock a few years less than that. César died convulsing, mouth filled with a thick yellow foam that the keeper nonchalantly said had come from eating 'something bad', while the peacock – what happened to the peacock? Its throat ripped open by a possum? An unexplained disappearance into thin air, leaving only glimmering blue-green feathers behind? Even five years ago he felt too exhausted to replace them, and it feels even less worth it now – it's just not the time and place for those sorts of things anymore, for that kind of exhibitionism. Not the right atmosphere. He walks on, the house getting smaller in the distance, the sounds of the party getting fainter, ignoring the dampness seeping into the hems of his trousers, the midge-bites forming on his arms.

We follow him as best we can. We tread carefully over the squashed mangoes and dark green chicken turds curled up like undiscovered Easter candy among the grass. We follow him past the fenced field, the one with the steer who always looks so sad, and never bothers to flick the flies away from its thick eyelashes. We pass the out-house with the backup electricity generator, the acacia tree where the buzzards roost. The ranch is over a thousand hectares long but he won't be going much farther.

We're just about to begin, when it happens. At first there's hardly any sound, the canopy barely rustling, trees shaking. We stand as still as possible as he turns around sharply, staring deep into the darkness around him. 'Sweetie?' he says. 'Is that you?'

The sound grows louder, leaves and twigs crashing down.

'Who's there?' His hand moves to his hip, towards the hidden holster. Fingers tensed and ready.

The monkey takes its last swing out of the tree, landing heavily on the ground. It straightens up, wet black eyes blinking. His fingers relax around the holster, but don't move away.

'Well,' he says. 'Hello there, old friend.'

Baloo doesn't even give him a glance. Instead, he stares right at us.

We stare back.

'Sorry I don't have anything for you,' he says. 'Any, ah, goodies.' He's touching his waist and back pockets, instinctively feeling for something, wishing he'd brought the flip-flop, or even the gnawed stick. His fingers suddenly detect the plastic baggie of JELL-O powder, which he immediately pulls out and throws in Baloo's direction. It flutters weakly like a translucent moth, landing near the monkey's foot. Baloo doesn't even flinch, his eyes still fixed unblinkingly on us. We shift around uncomfortably, glancing at each other, nervously crossing and uncrossing our arms. Some of us tentatively touch our cheeks and foreheads, tracing the skin with our fingertips.

It's almost like he's saying: *What's wrong with your faces?*

Or even: *Wait – what did they do to you?*

'Good monkey,' he says, backing away, one slow but steady footstep at a time. 'Nice little Baloo.' In response Baloo releases a long lazy yawn, flashing a row of solid yellow teeth. His breath is warm and stinks of overripe fruit.

The cellphone rings, its high-pitched trill breaking the silence, and we can't help but jump as Baloo swiftly turns and flees into the undergrowth, bushes rattling like chattering teeth. He fumbles with the cellphone as he pulls it out, fingers clumsy, answers just before it goes to voicemail. At first he thinks it's Nicolás from the processing laboratory, speaking rapidly in muffled tones, but finally recognises prostate-cancer Andrés – he's agitated, calling long-distance from Medellín, asking repeatedly if it's safe to speak right now. He listens calmly to the update, strolling back towards the house. He interrupts with a stifled snort of laughter, after Andrés says, *My advice would be for you to take a trip abroad for a while – with your daughter especially. Why risk it? Go to Europe; take her someplace nice. Just until things blow over with these guys. Until the situation is safe again.*

'We're not going anywhere,' he says, cutting Andrés off. 'I don't care what you have to do. Just take care of it.'

The walk back to the house feels strangely short. Right as he passes the flip-flop he pauses, as if about to bend over and scoop it up, but at the last second he turns quickly away, leaving it behind in the grass. The party's now reached the point where it's either going to turn into anarchy or collapse into exhausted decay. Somebody's thrown up on the grass, a sour orange puddle. The dancers and drinkers on the patio are still mingling, eyes glassy, cheeks stiff from smiling. Somebody's turned the music up so loud that the bass hurts his eardrums.

He's heading towards the patio door when he's spotted. *Hey, there you are! Where have you been hiding?* He's reluctantly tugged away, pulled into the crowd. His shoulders are slapped, his arms are squeezed, he receives winks and smiles, shouts and whoops. A shot of *aguardiente,* miraculously still cold, is pushed into his hand, followed by delicate kisses on his cheek. *Terrific party! Amazing! Best time I've had since Carnival!*

Everybody's happy to see him; they're thrilled that he's here. He briefly scans the crowd one last time, but there are no children to be seen at this point – no small bowed heads, no hands stained with hardened candle wax, no wet chewed braid. The phone sits in his back pocket, still warm from the call.

He checks his messages one more time from the quietest corner of the patio, under the grapefruit tree by the swimming pool. There are no new voicemails. Not even a text.

He's walking past the swimming pool when he sees it: the last paper plate, bobbing up and down, half-sunken. Its candle is long gone, most likely sunk to the bottom, now rolling slowly across the tiles. The pool is completely dark; there's no longer any light to be seen. He stops and watches.

There are more packages of paper plates deep inside the pantry somewhere. He could go ask a maid to bring more out. Or even better, he could get them himself. Take the key off the chain, unlock the door, head inside. If he wanted to, he could spend some time slumped on the floor, leaning against the wall, eyes closed, hands resting calmly in lap. It could be the kind of place where he could stay forever. Stay secret. Stay safe. A place where he could lock himself away and never, ever be found.

We'll be watching, though. We don't mind. We're not in a hurry.

We're not going anywhere.

42

Julianne Pachico grew up in Colombia and now lives in Norwich, where she is completing her PhD in Creative and Critical Writing at UEA. Her stories have been published by *New Writing.net* and *Lighthouse Literary Journal.* She is currently completing her first collection of linked stories.

To find out more about Daunt Books
publications and to subscribe to our
newsletter, please visit
www.dauntbooks.co.uk.